Little Bird's First Adventure

Written by
Meghan Fife *Meghan Fife 6/12/06*

Illustrations by Andrew Fife and Julio Badel

Andrew Fife 6/12/06

First published by AuthorHouse 2/22/2006

ISBN: 1-4208-5071-7

Printed in the United States of America
Bloomington, Indiana

This book is printed on acid-free paper.

authorHOUSE

1663 LIBERTY DRIVE
BLOOMINGTON, INDIANA 47403
(800) 839-8640
www.authorhouse.com

For Nicolas, Timothy and Nina

This is the story of Little Bird and his very first adventure.

Little Bird was a very young sparrow that had finally grown his feathers and was getting ready to leave the nest.

One day Little Bird found himself all alone, for his brothers and sisters had already left the nest.

He knew that it would be his time to leave as well, and soon enough Mother Bird reminded Little Bird that he too must fly from the nest.

Little Bird was scared to fly, but Mother Bird encouraged him until Little Bird finally made that first jump.

Mother Bird chirped with excitement as she watched Little Bird spread his wings to fly, but Little Bird did not fly.

He bounced from one branch to the next all the way down the tree until he landed on the hard ground below. Ouch! Little Bird was now confused, and sat wondering about what to do next.

A little girl walking home from school noticed Little Bird on the ground next to the tree. She quietly came close to him, looked down, and whispered, "Oh, you poor little bird. You must have fallen from your nest."

The little girl gently picked up the little bird and placed him in an old box she found nearby. Next, she put a small plastic bowl of water in the box and tried to feed him soggy bread from her lunch box, but Little Bird wasn't used to such food. He was used to Mother Bird feeding him worms and did not know what to do with the soggy bread and water that was in the box. Little Bird did not eat. Instead, he began to chirp very loudly, calling for his mother.

He continued to chirp, hoping that she would hear him and rescue him, but Mother Bird could not hear him, for Little Bird was now far away from his nest and the tree.

The little girl had taken Little Bird back to her house where she asked her mother what to do, but her mother did not know. Little Bird stared up from the box, wishing he could tell them what to do. "Please take me back to my nest where Mother Bird will take care of me!" he chirped, but the little girl did not understand, and just looked at him and sighed, "Poor little bird, what can we do to help you?"

The little girl telephoned a wildlife rescue center and found the answers to her questions. She was told that because Little Bird had all of his feathers and did not appear to be hurt, he was probably a fledgling who had just left the nest and was learning to fly.

Since many fledglings continue to run and hop on the ground while learning to fly, he needed more time to practice flying. Just like when the little girl was first learning to walk, and needed to practice and sometimes would fall before she was able to walk on her own, Little Bird needed to practice running, hopping and jumping before he would be able to fly on his own.

Mother Bird would continue to care for him, so it was best to return Little Bird to his tree. The little girl wondered if Mother Bird might reject Little Bird since human hands had touched him, but because most birds cannot smell very well, Mother Bird would never know so he would be just fine.

The little girl quickly returned Little Bird to the tree where she had found him. Little Bird was now quiet and sat wondering about what was going to happen next.

As he looked up from the box, he noticed the familiar leaves on the trees and the blue sky above. Little Bird was overjoyed, and began chirping very loudly for his Mother Bird. "Mother! Mother! I'm here! I'm here!"

The little girl looked up at the tree and noticed the nest that Little Bird must have jumped from. She wanted to return him to his nest where he would be safe, but the nest was much too high for her to climb to. She climbed up to the lowest branch she could reach and carefully placed the box in the tree. She then said goodbye to Little Bird and wished him well.

Little Bird continued to chirp ever more loudly, calling out to his mother. As the little girl watched from the ground, she saw that Mother Bird had finally heard him, and flew around the tree chirping back at her Little Bird.

At last, Mother Bird landed on top of the box with a fresh worm for Little Bird. Suddenly the chirping stopped, as now Little Bird was safe at home, no longer scared or hungry.

Mother Bird continued to fly in and out of the box, feeding her Little Bird and encouraging him once again to take his first flight.

A few days passed and the little girl returned to the tree where she had found Little Bird. She looked up to see that the old box was still in the same place where she had left it, but this time Little Bird was perched on top of the box, with a few more feathers than he had before.

She watched quietly as Little Bird looked around. He then looked down at her for just a moment, perhaps to say thank you, before quickly leaping from the box, spreading his wings, and soaring high into the blue sky.

Little Bird had finally made his first flight, and he didn't come back down this time.

The little girl smiled to herself as she watched Little Bird disappear from sight. She knew in her heart that Little Bird would be just fine, for he had already survived his first adventure.

ABOUT THE AUTHOR

Meghan Fife was born and raised in Southern California, where she currently lives and works as a middle school teacher. Writing remains one of her many passions, as well as world travel and photography. She also volunteers for various organizations dedicated to the care and well being of the natural environment and its inhabitants. She would like to thank her illustrators for their dedicated talent and support, as well as the real little bird that inspired this story.